Topsy and Tim
Halloween Party

By Jean and Gareth Adamson

LADYBIRD BOOKS

UK | USA | Canada | Ireland | Australia
India | New Zealand | South Africa

Ladybird Books is part of the Penguin Random House group of companies
whose addresses can be found at global.penguinrandomhouse.com
www.penguin.co.uk   www.puffin.co.uk   www.ladybird.co.uk

First published 2019
001

Printed in China

A CIP catalogue record for this book is available from the British Library

ISBN: 978–0–241–38616–3

All correspondence to:
Ladybird Books
Penguin Random House Children's
80 Strand, London WC2R 0RL

This Topsy and Tim book belongs to

When Topsy and Tim looked out of the window early one October morning, they saw something big and white flapping in the garden.

"Look!" said Topsy. "It's a ghost!"
Then Tim remembered something. "It's Halloween!"
Topsy and Tim were having a Halloween party, and all their friends were invited.

In the kitchen, two plump pumpkins sat side by side, one for Topsy and one for Tim.

After breakfast, Dad showed Topsy and Tim how to make Halloween lanterns. They drew spooky faces on the pumpkins, then Dad cut the tops off so the twins could scoop out the insides. Next, he carefully cut out the faces they had drawn, and put a safe little light inside each one.

"These lanterns will glow nicely in the dark," said Dad.

Stumpy, their pet mouse, was watching. Tim dropped some pumpkin into Stumpy's bowl. Then he helped Topsy put the lanterns on the windowsill.

Mummy was standing on a chair with a tangle
of fairy lights. On the floor was a bag full of
soft, fluffy white stuff. Tim pulled a bit out.
It was very stretchy.
Tim wrapped some round Topsy.
"It's tickly!" she laughed.

"Hoy!" said Mummy. "Those are my cobwebs!"
They unwrapped Topsy and draped the cobwebs round
the room instead.

There was a lot of party food to get ready.
Topsy and Tim made:

maggoty apples

mummy rolls

spiderweb pizzas

frozen ghost lollies

and pumpkin cookies.

At last it was time for the party. Topsy and Tim were dressed in their Halloween costumes. Topsy was a witch and Tim was a skeleton.

Topsy and Tim's friends were all dressed up, too. Tony Welch was a spider, Kerry was a witch's cat and Stevie Dunton was a pirate. Last to arrive was Andy Anderson, dressed as a giant pumpkin.

"Wow!" said Kerry. "We're in a magic haunted house!"

Soon the children were chasing around, cackling like witches and *whooo*-ing like ghosts. Andy watched them. He was feeling a little bit nervous.

"Who'd like to play a game?" called Mummy.

The first game was called Wrapping Mummies, but this was a different sort of mummy! The two teams raced as fast as they could to wrap Tony and Kerry from top to toe in toilet paper.

Soon *nearly* everyone was laughing.
What a mess!

Mummy and Dad held tight to the ends of a long, strong piece of string. Dangling from the string were lots of doughnuts.

"I might need someone to help me hold this steady," said Dad to Andy.

Topsy, Tim and their friends tried to eat the doughnuts without using their hands. It was harder than it looked. Soon there were crumbs all over the floor!

While Dad swept up, everyone danced to funny monster music. Each time the music stopped, they had to stand as still as statues, without wobbling or giggling.

Next was a game called Apple Bobbing. Apples floated in a bowl of water, and everyone tried to catch one with their teeth. They all got a bit wet!

"You lot won't need baths tonight!" said Mummy.

It was time for a story. Topsy, Tim and their friends sat down while Mummy told a tale about a witch and her magic potion.

As Mummy told the story, the children put their hands into the witch's cauldron. They squealed as they felt dried rats' tails, crunchy beetles and a tangle of sticky worms! Andy did not want to put his hand in at all.

At the end of the story, Mummy taught them all a magic spell.
"Eye of frog and beetles' feet, turn into something good to eat!"

"Go on!" said Topsy to Andy. "See if the spell worked."
"Shall I do it with you?" asked Tim.
They both put their hands into the cauldron
and pulled out . . . delicious chocolate!
"I liked that trick!" said Andy,
munching his chocolate happily.

There was a loud knock at the front door.
"Is it home time?" wondered Dad.

Standing on the doorstep was a gaggle of giggling ghosts and
ghouls. They had seen Topsy and Tim's pumpkins grinning at
the window, so they knew it would be all right to knock.

"Trick or treat!" they shouted.

Luckily, there were plenty of chocolate frogs left in the
witch's cooking pot for all the spooky visitors to have a treat.
"Thank you!" they said, as they helped themselves and went
on their way.

"Tea's ready!" called Mummy.

"It looks like a skeletons' banquet!" said Tim.

Kerry's napkin fell off the table. It began to shuffle across the floor all by itself.

"Oh no!" said Topsy. "It must be a ghost!"

Topsy bravely lifted the napkin. It was Stumpy the mouse!
Tim had forgotten to close the cage door at breakfast time.
Topsy gently put Stumpy back in his cage, and Tim made sure
the door was shut tightly this time.

There were more knocks at the door, but this time it wasn't
trick-or-treaters. It was mums and dads.
It really was home time now.

That night, as Topsy and Tim lay tucked up in their beds, two pumpkins glowed softly in the dark beside them.

"I wish it was Halloween again tomorrow," said Tim to Topsy.

But Topsy was already fast asleep, and then so was Tim.

*Now turn the page and help
Topsy and Tim solve a puzzle.*

Topsy, Tim and Mummy are decorating their house for Halloween. Can you spot the five differences between these two scenes?

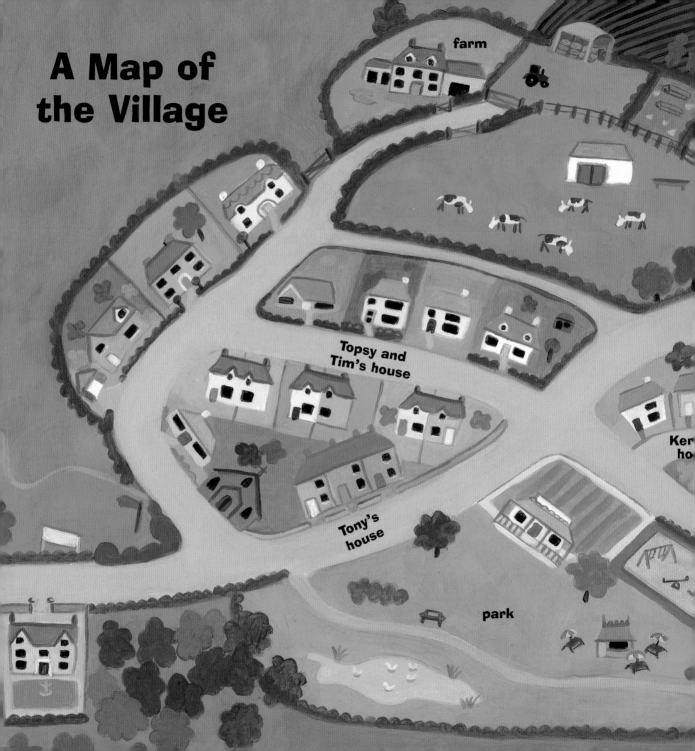

A Map of the Village

farm

Topsy and
Tim's house

Tony's
house

Ker
ho

park

garage

post
office

health
centre

church

primary school

nursery school

police station

Have you read all the Topsy and Tim stories?

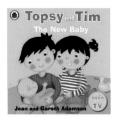 The New Baby
9781409300564

 Have a Birthday Party
9781409300618

 Go on an Aeroplane
9781409300571

 Play Football
9781409303350

 Go on a Train
9781409304241

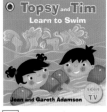 Learn to Swim
9781409300601

 Start School
9781409300830

 Go Camping
9781409303336

 Go to Hospital
9781409304234

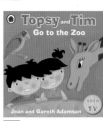 Go to the Zoo
9781409300847

 Go to the Dentist
9781409300588

 At the Farm
9781409303367

 Go to the Doctor
9781409303343

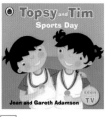 Have Itchy Heads
9781409307204

 Meet the Firefighters
9781409307211

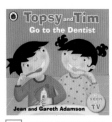 Safety First
9781409308829

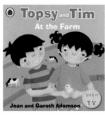 Meet the Police
9781409308836

 Sports Day
9781409309468

 Visit London
9781409309475

 Meet Father Christmas
9781409311591

 Help a Friend
9780723292593

 Move House
9780723292586

 Go on Holiday
9780241282557

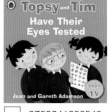 Have Their Eyes Tested
9780241282540

 Halloween Party
✓ 9780241386163